Sisters in the Air

Louise McPhetridge Thaden
Aviation Record Holder
National Aviation Hall of Fame Inductee

Phoebe Fairgrave Omlie
First Lady of Aviation in Tennessee

Helen DeWitt Whittaker

The Overmountain Press
JOHNSON CITY, TENNESSEE

Dedicated to my mother, Margaret, who always wanted to publish; to my daughter, Elizabeth, who probably will; and to my husband, Gary, who gives me ideas, encouragement, and adventures to write about.

ISBN 1-57072-229-3
Copyright © 2002 by Helen DeWitt Whittaker
All Rights Reserved
Printed in the United States of America

1 2 3 4 5 6 7 8 9 0

Prologue

Louise McPhetridge Thaden and Phoebe Fairgrave Omlie were both born in the early 1900s. They met each other when Louise was 23 and Phoebe was 26—on an airfield. It was 1929, and the women were two of 100 licensed female pilots in the country as well as two of the competitors in the first all-women's air race.

During their lives, they both won many air races and set several aviation records. Louise received honors for her aviation achievements, including induction into the National Aviation Hall of Fame in Dayton, Ohio. Phoebe also received various honors, including the naming of the control tower, the Omlie Tower, at the Memphis International Airport in Tennessee.

These are the incredible stories of two remarkable women who became sisters in the air.

Louise at the Bendix Race. *Louise McPhetridge Thaden collection, National Air and Space Museum, Smithsonian Institution (SI Neg. No. 79-7387)*

Louise McPhetridge Thaden

Iris Louise McPhetridge was born on November 12, 1905, in Bentonville, Arkansas. The older of two girls, Louise was a typical tomboy who enjoyed hunting and fishing with her father. Her parents, Roy Fry and Edna Hobbs McPhetridge, had no idea their daughter would grow up to be a record-setting pilot and an extraordinary role model for young girls. In fact, flying was a foreign idea to Roy and Edna. The Wright Brothers had made their first powered flight in 1903, only two years earlier. Their newfangled flying machines were viewed as oddities that would never last.

Louise's love of aviation blossomed early when, at age 7, she jumped off the barn roof holding an oversized umbrella. She thought it was great fun. But she had to wait until her college years before she actually had an opportunity to fly in an airplane.

After graduating from Bentonville High School at age 15, Louise attended the University of Arkansas. She never could settle down to her studies and switched majors from journalism to physical education, and then to premed. She interrupted her education twice.

The first time, she left school to work for a year at the J. H. Turner Coal Company in Wichita, Kansas. During the work week she sold coal, fuel oil, and building material, but on the weekends she hung out at a nearby airplane factory, the Travel Air Factory. There she watched the airplanes and occasionally obtained rides from the workers.

She played hooky from work one day to watch the planes, and her boss, Mr. Turner, caught her there. She just knew she was going to be fired, but instead he recognized her sincere interest in aviation and decided to encourage her. Mr. Turner was a stockholder of the Travel Air Factory and knew the owner, Walter Beech. He introduced Louise to Mr. Beech, and a year later, when Louise left the university for the second time, Mr. Beech hired her.

He sent her to San Francisco to work for his West Coast distributor, D. C. Warren. During the day Louise typed, and in the evenings she took flying lessons. She first flew solo in 1927, and soon after that she began flying demonstration planes for Travel Air. When she had accumulated 5 hours and 15 minutes of solo time, she received her Federation Aeronautique Internationale (FAI) Aviators certificate. It was signed by none other than Orville

Wright. By being in the air almost all of her free time, Louise soon accumulated the 200 hours of solo time she needed to apply for a Transport Pilot rating. She took a ground-school course and passed the written test. All that remained for her to do was pass the flight test.

As she climbed into the plane with the inspector who would judge her flying, she was informed that he was going to be extra hard on her because he didn't want to take the blame for any crashes she might have. This made Louise furious, and as a result she flew the best she'd ever flown. She passed with flying colors and became the fourth woman in the United States to receive the classification of Transport Pilot rating.

In the midst of all her working and flying, Louise met a former U.S. Army pilot and aeronautical engineer by the name of Herbert Von Thaden. They fell in love and eloped to Reno on July 2, 1928. Herbert soon found that he had married an unusual woman for the times. She liked to work, she loved to fly, and, as he was soon to discover, she liked to compete.

On December 7, 1928, at the Oakland Airport in California, Louise set out to establish the first altitude record for women. In those pioneer days of aviation, the pilots didn't have much equipment to help them. Most of the cockpits were open, and there were no pressurized cabins or oxygen masks. In fact, Louise fashioned her breathing apparatus from a cylinder of oxygen she obtained from a

Louise is prepared for a high-altitude flight. *Louise McPhetridge Thaden collection, National Air and Space Museum, Smithsonian Institution (SI Neg. No. 83-2158)*

machine shop. She used a rubber hose to connect a hospital ether mask to the cylinder and controlled the valves by turning them with a pair of pliers. There is no doubt that it was a risky flight.

She flew one of Mr. Beech's Travel Airs with 180 horsepower. Although the ground temperature in Oakland was 87 degrees, she wore a fur-lined flying suit to keep her warm at the higher elevations, where it could become as cold as 24 degrees below zero.

Louise later said that she made it up to 27,000 feet, and then she passed out. She woke up at 16,200 feet and brought the plane in safely. The official reading on her barograph was 20,260 feet. It took Louise 1 hour and 38 minutes to establish the first official altitude record for women in the United States.

Louise was no longer the indecisive teenager with an interest in flying. She was a vocal, compassionate woman with an evangelical belief in aviation. As she wrote in her autobiography, "Flight is abiding peace. Absolute serenity. It is faith and compassion. Purest joy. It is spirit totally free. Flight is yesterday's yearning. The fulfillment of today's dreams. Tomorrow's promises."[1]

Not only did she love flying, but she also loved to push her limits. She really pushed them in 1929 by breaking two more aviation records and winning the first women's air race.

In March of 1929, Louise donned riding pants, boots, leather jacket, helmet, and goggles to climb into another Travel Air at the Oakland Airport in California. Female pilots usually wore either skirts or riding pants (jodhpurs) to fly. Since most of the cockpits were open, they wore goggles and a helmet as well. If they flew on sunny days, their faces would look like raccoons when they removed their goggles. If they flew on rainy days, their skin would literally sting from the driving force of the rain.

That day in March was sunny and perfect for flying. Louise took her plane up around 4:00 in the afternoon in an attempt to set a new solo endurance record for women. She had to fly in circles above the airport, which quickly became boring. She managed to stay alert by singing, whistling, and chewing gum. Flying during the night was especially difficult, since she was tired and there wasn't much to hold her interest in order to help keep her alert.

By morning, planes were taking off from the airport below and flying up to offer encouragement. At one point during her flight she did nod off, only to be immediately awakened by a loud thud. The spinner on her propeller had fallen off and hit the tail of the plane. That was certainly enough to get her adrenaline pumping.

Louise managed to fly until the afternoon, landing after 22 hours, 3 minutes, and 28 seconds. She established a new solo endurance record for women.

Not one to rest on her laurels, she decided to go for another record the next month—this time for speed. She was again at the Oakland Airport in another Travel Air, built especially for the event by Mr. Beech. She had to make two runs across the airport at no more than 300 feet off the ground.

When a pilot is flying very high, the sense of speed is minimal. But when a pilot flies low to the ground—like at 300 feet—everything on the ground seems to zoom by. She wrote, "I was exalted with speed, with swift, powerful, unobstructed flight, cutting the air with knife-edge ease. Mastery, accomplishment, freedom, ego; verve, vitality; I was ready to burst with the joy of being so thoroughly alive—for the ability to fly."[2]

Enthralled with this sense of fantastic speed, Louise pushed herself and her plane to the limit, setting a new record of 156 miles per hour. The day she set the record, she became the first and only woman ever to hold simultaneous records for speed, altitude, and solo endurance.

As incredible as her records were, Louise wasn't finished making history. For several years, a prestigious National Air Race had been held in Cleveland, Ohio. The female pilots, especially Amelia Earhart, had been trying to get the men to let the women compete in the National Air Race. Rather than granting their request, the race officials allowed the women to organize an all-female race that would be held in conjunction with the Cleveland race, finishing in Cleveland. It was formally called the National Women's Air Derby but was nicknamed the Powder Puff Derby.

The women were thrilled to get their own race.

For years they had been wanting to prove to the public that they were serious pilots, not just cute salesgirls for motor oil and gas. By 1929, there were almost a hundred female pilots in the United States.

The entrants had to meet certain qualifications. They had to hold a license issued by the Department of Commerce. They had to have logged 100 hours of solo time, 25 of which had to be in cross-country flights of more than 40 miles. They also had to hold an FAI license and an annual sporting license that was issued by the contest committee of the National Aeronautical Association.

At the time, only 40 female pilots met those requirements. Of those, 23 registered to enter the race. Three women withdrew before the race began, leaving 20 competitors.

The entrants in this historic race came from all walks of life. Some were college graduates. Some had wealthy families. Some ran their own businesses. Some earned money as barnstormers performing stunt flying at county fairs and carnivals. Some of the women were homemakers, and two were mothers. Others gave up promising careers in journalism, music, and the theater, while a few of them already had aviation careers as airplane saleswomen and Hollywood stunt pilots. No matter what their differences, they all shared one love—flying.

The race began on Sunday, August 18, in Santa Monica, California, and was scheduled to end on Monday, August 26, in Cleveland, Ohio. The route was: Santa Monica, San Bernardino, California;

Yuma, Phoenix, Douglas, Arizona; El Paso, Pecos, Midland, Abilene, Fort Worth, Texas; Tulsa, Oklahoma; Wichita, Kansas City, Kansas; East St. Louis, Missouri; Terre Haute, Indiana; Cincinnati, Columbus, and Cleveland, Ohio.

The pilots were required to fly stock factory models with no special installations. There were two categories: light planes and heavy planes. Louise was in the heavy plane category. The prize money was to be divided between the two groups.

Most of the women reached Santa Monica the day before the race in anticipation of attending the highly publicized aviation ball being held that night. The women walked into the ballroom in their evening gowns, gloves, cloches, pearls, and heels. One small difference between the female pilots and the other women was that the next morning, the pilots would pull on unionalls, jodhpurs, helmets, and goggles to climb into machines that they would fly over 2,000 miles of unknown terrain.

On Sunday, August 18, the early-morning air still had a chill in it. Cars crowded onto the grassy fields. There was an undercurrent of excitement in the air. Prior to takeoff, the women were reminded to wear a parachute and to carry one gallon of drinking water, a three-day supply of malted milk tablets, and beef jerky. Since those were pioneer days in aviation, it wasn't unusual to have to bail out of a plane or land unexpectedly. Forced landings and occasional crashes were considered normal. Therefore, it was important to carry food and water along. Some women also brought chewing gum, tomato juice, and oranges to wet their parched throats and keep them alert during monotonous hops.

Flying conditions were primitive compared to today's technological advancements. There was no radio contact with anyone. No instruments were available to tell them their speed or direction. The women had to navigate by dead reckoning, using only temperamental compasses, stopwatches, and road maps. Paved runways were few and far between. Many communities plowed landing strips out of fields, and three of the destinations in the race had never before received airplanes.

The competition participants other than Louise Thaden were Amelia Earhart, the first woman to cross the Atlantic; Phoebe Omlie, a stunt pilot in the *Perils of Pauline* movies; Jessie Maude Keith-Miller, the first woman to fly from London to Australia; Claire Mae Fahy, whose husband, Lt. Herbert J. Fahy, set the solo record for men; Thea Rasche, an internationally known German pilot; Evelyn "Bobbi" Trout, a Hollywood stunt pilot; Edith Foltz, a barnstormer; Mae Haizlip, whose husband was a WWI pilot who ran a flying school; Marvel Crosson, an Alaskan aviation business owner; Florence Lowe "Pancho" Barnes, a stunt pilot in *Hell's Angels*; Blanche Wilcox Noyes, who had flown solo only six months prior to the race; Margaret Perry, a commercial pilot; Ruth Rowland Nichols, a former flying boat pilot who flew the first nonstop flight from New

Waiting for bad weather to clear at Parks Airport, East St. Louis, during the 1929 women's air race are (left to right) Mary Von Mach, Jessie Keith-Miller, Gladys O'Donnell, Thea Rasche, Phoebe Omlie, Louise Thaden, Amelia Earhart, Blanche Noyes, Ruth Elder, and Vera Walker. *Louise McPhetridge Thaden collection, National Air and Space Museum, Smithsonian Institution (SI Neg. No. 89-21987)*

York to Miami; Opal Logan Kunz, a wealthy socialite whose husband was a vice president at Tiffany; Neva Paris, an aviation saleswoman for Curtiss-Wright; Ruth Elder, an actress; Gladys Berry O'Donnell, a pylon racer; Mary Von Mach, who flew for fun; and Vera Dawn Walker, who, at 4'11", had to prop herself up on pillows to reach the rudder pedals.

When the women assembled for the Derby, they did not meet as competitors. They met as comrades and sisters. Although a few of them knew each other from previous aviation events, most of them met that day for the first time. It was a significant personal and historical experience. They were all determined to fly a successful race.

As the women prepared themselves in their cockpits for the start of nine grueling days, they experienced many emotions. As Louise best expressed it, they were pilots "with dry mouths, wild pumping hearts, sweating hands fumbling over maps, controls, adjusting goggles, unreasoning speculation. Hope, determination, a feeling of history in the making with each one playing a part. Adventure, youth, soaring carefree on wings of romance; intoxicated, happy, thrilled, suffocated in rapture."[3]

She flew a Travel Air plane that Walter Beech had built especially for her and the competition. When Louise picked up her new plane in Wichita, Kansas, Mr. Beech insisted on following her to Fort Worth, Texas, to make sure everything went smoothly. New planes frequently had problems that didn't become apparent until they had been flown a few hours. Mr. Beech got to Fort Worth first and waited anxiously for Louise to come.

When she came in view of the runway, she flew straight in, rather than circling the airport, as was her usual custom. Mr. Beech became convinced something was wrong, because she also landed too fast. He was right.

She stumbled out of the plane covered in black soot from the exhaust fumes, then collapsed. Later, she awoke and was informed that she had carbon monoxide poisoning. Mr. Beech ran a pipe with a funnel at the end from the cowling into the cockpit so she could breathe fresh air. She flew the rest of the way to California, as well as the entire Derby, with her face pressed to the funnel.

The conditions of the race were far from ideal. Landing was especially hazardous at times because of low visibility due to shimmering heat waves or dust-covered runways. Amelia Earhart nosed over once when landing, due to poor visibility caused by the extreme heat. Two other pilots crashed into vehicles that were parked too close to the landing strip.

Louise got caught in some violent turbulence that almost lifted her out of her cockpit. She hit her head and shattered her goggles, but she managed to maintain control of her plane. She also had difficulty finding an airport during a particularly bad storm. The pelting rain turned her windshield into an opaque wall, so she had to lean out into the wind and stinging rain to spot the runway.

Another more serious problem for the racers was sabotage. Someone cut the brace wires on Claire Fahy's plane, taking her out of the race. Thea Rasche found sand in her gas tank. And someone filed the breaker points on both magnetos in Louise's plane.

Tragedy struck when Marvel Crosson crashed and died. Louise and Marvel had become close friends, and Louise was shaken up when she heard the news. Louise became angry when the men, who didn't approve of the women racing anyway, tried to use Marvel's crash as a reason to halt the race. Fatalities in men's races were considered occupational hazards, but in women's races they were viewed as signs of incompetence. As the president of Safeway Air Lines said, "The Women's Air Derby is contributing nothing to aviation and should be cancelled immediately. . . . Women are lacking certain qualities concerning aviation. Handling details essential to safe flying is one of the qualifications women have not mastered successfully. Women have been dependent on men for guidance for so long that when they are put on their own resources, they are handicapped."[4]

The women read the headlines calling for a halt to the race, but they didn't let the negative comments stop them. They knew the importance of what they were doing. They needed to finish the race not only for themselves, but also for every woman who had flown or who would someday fly.

Louise waves to the crowd moments after her win of the 1929 women's air race. *Louise McPhetridge Thaden collection, National Air and Space Museum, Smithsonian Institution (SI Neg. No. 89-22002)*

As Louise expressed it, "If your time has come to go, it is a glorious way in which to cross over. Smell of burning oil, the feel of strength and power beneath your hands. So quick has been the transition from life to death, there must still linger in your mind's eye the everlasting beauty and joy of flight. Fear and terror rear ugly heads only when there is time to think. We women pilots were blazing a new trail. Each pioneering effort must bow to death. There has never been nor will there ever be progress without sacrifice of human life. Although the women accepted the possible consequences of injury or death, the media called for them to stop the race. But the women wanted to finish. To us the successful completion of the Derby was of more import than life or death."[5]

Twenty women had started the race in Santa Monica. Only fourteen departed Columbus, Ohio, for the final hop to Cleveland. When the women arrived, the crowd of over 40,000 spectators went wild. Reporters and photographers swarmed the planes. Louise was the first in, winning the race with an official time of 20 hours, 20 minutes, and 2 seconds. Her plane was pushed across the field in front of the stands. She was adorned with a horseshoe of flowers, which she put on her plane. Gladys O'Donnell was second in the heavy plane category. Amelia Earhart was third and Blanche Noyes was fourth. Phoebe Omlie finished first in the light plane category and fifth in total time.

Louise's words of victory reflected her belief in the

ability of all the women: "I'm glad to be here. All the girls flew a splendid race, much better than I. Each one deserves first place because each one is a winner. Mine is a faster ship. Thank you."[6]

The comradery of the women was evident in Blanche Noyes's comments about the race. "It was a wonderful, wonderful experience. I'm so glad that I had the chance to know the other girls in the race. I became especially acquainted with Louise Thaden, Amelia Earhart and Phoebe Omlie because our rooms were always near each other and each night we'd gather in one of our rooms to talk over the day."[7]

In spite of all the controversy surrounding the race, it had the "highest per cent of 'finishers' in any cross country derby, up to that time, for men or women."[8]

The women proved they could fly, and they proved to the men that they were competent. They won the country's admiration and respect for their abilities, finally achieving the recognition they longed for.

After the completion of the race, Louise and her new friend Amelia Earhart decided they should organize the female pilots in order to foster fellowship and inspiration. Ninety-nine women responded to their invitation, so they called themselves The Ninety-Nines. Louise was asked to be the first president, but she felt that Amelia was better known and therefore would attract more recognition for the women.

In 1930, a group in Pittsburgh purchased Herb's

airplane factory. Herb and Louise moved to Pittsburgh, where he worked for the new owners and she took a position with the Pennsylvania School of Aviation as director of the women's division. She was also director of public relations for the Pittsburgh Aviation Industries Corp.

In the summer of 1930, Louise added another demanding role to her life when she became a mother. She gave birth to a son, William, and three years later she had a daughter, Patricia. The early years of motherhood put a hiatus on her flying. She missed it and thought housework was tedious. As she explained in her autobiography, "I missed the soothing splendor of flight. The ability to go up into God's heaven, to look out toward distant horizons, to gaze down upon the struggling creatures far below, to forget troubles which so short a time before seemed staggering, just to feel the lifting of the wheels from the ground, to hear the rush of air past the cabin window, to squint into the sun, toying with the controls, to feel the exhilaration of power under taut leash, responsible to whim or fancy, to feel, if only for one brief moment, that I could be master of my fate—that is what I missed."[9]

By 1932, she couldn't stand sitting at home anymore. The Thadens had moved to Baltimore. A friend asked Louise to set a new refueling record. Louise asked Frances Marsalis, a pilot friend, to assist her. Neither of the women knew anything about refueling flights, but they were willing to learn.

They took a Curtiss Thrush airplane, removed

Louise and Frances refuel during their record-setting endurance flight. *National Air and Space Museum, Smithsonian Institution (SI Neg. No. 79-7393)*

all the seats, and ripped the rug off the floor. They loaded gallon tins of engine oil, grease, tools, parachutes, spare engine parts, medical supplies, an air mattress, cosmetics, clean clothes, and thermos bottles of hot coffee and water onto the plane.

The refueling plane would hover above, drop a hose, and pump fuel to them. It also would drop them their food, clothes, and spare parts via a basket lowered on a rope.

After flying for only 18 hours, they had to land because they broke contact with the refueling plane too soon, tearing off the left wingtip. It was repaired, and they returned to the air. Louise and Frances flew in four-hour shifts for the first two days, then three-hour shifts, and then two-hour shifts.

Their flight circuit above Curtiss Field in Long Island, New York, was boring. The women just traveled in a circle and tried to stay alert. Their air mattress was punctured on day two, so they slept on the hard metal floor and used an oil can for a pillow. They washed with rubbing alcohol and cotton.

On day six a storm developed, forcing them to fly extremely low—below 100 feet—through most of the night. By the eighth day, they had had about all the fun they could handle, so Louise landed. They set a new women's refueling record for 196 hours with 78 air-to-air refueling contacts.

Two years later, in 1934, Louise went to work for the Bureau of Air Commerce with Phoebe Omlie, another Powder Puff Derby contestant. Their job was to promote the marking of airfields and landmarks nationwide. As a result, Louise and Phoebe developed and organized the National Air Marking Program. They enlisted the aid of three other female pilots.

At the time, most pilots flew without radios, so they couldn't contact a tower to ask where they were. Pilots relied mainly on Rand McNally road maps. The Air Marking program identified prominent buildings in towns across the country in order to paint the towns' names on the roofs. Louise worked with this program until 1936.

During the 1930s, the Cleveland Air Races were the major aviation events in the world. The Powder Puff Derby was a part of this event, but the highlight of the program was the Bendix Transcontinental Air Race. The winner's purse from that race was the largest offered in aviation.

It was first opened to women in 1935, but in 1936 a separate "consolation" prize of $2,500 was offered for the first woman to finish, because men assumed a woman couldn't possibly win the race. Olive Ann Beech, Walter's wife, asked Louise to fly in it, and Louise jumped at the chance. She asked Blanche Noyes to be her copilot.

The race began at Floyd Bennett Field in New York and ended in Los Angeles. Mr. Beech provided Louise with a stock airplane, not a racing plane. Louise and Blanche held no illusions that they would beat the racing planes, but they were excited about the possibility of winning the consolation prize.

Their Beech Staggerwing airplane was outfitted with an extra 56-gallon gas tank. They carried with

Louise stands with Blanche Noyes prior to the Bendix Race. *Louise McPhetridge Thaden collection, National Air and Space Museum, Smithsonian Institution (SI Neg. No. 77-4170)*

them maps, thermos bottles of water, concentrated food, flashlights, parachutes, chewing gum, sunglasses, handkerchiefs, a medicine kit, ammonia, scratch pads, pencils, matches, and a flare pistol. They were so cramped inside that Louise didn't think they would be able to squeeze out the door in their parachutes, even if they had to.

Each Bendix participant determined his or her own departure time. The only requirement was to arrive in Los Angeles no later than 6:00 p.m. Louise and Blanche were planning to get some sleep and then take off around dawn, but they couldn't rest because they were wound up with excitement. The distracting noise of other airplane departures during the night also kept them awake. They finally scrambled out of bed and took off around 4:00 a.m.

Flying conditions were far from ideal. An early-morning ground fog obscured their landmarks, and their radio wasn't working, so they had to fly a dead reckoning course using their maps, compass, and stopwatch. When they finally broke clear of the fog, they found an air marker (courtesy of Louise and Phoebe's program!) and discovered they were only 10 miles off course.

They were doing about 211 miles per hour when a violent thunderstorm developed, which cut their speed to 153 miles per hour. The headwinds were so strong and slowed them down so much that they didn't think they would make the 6:00 deadline. During the race the winds were so turbulent that the wings were ripped off of one contestant's plane, and another lost a propeller.

Louise and Blanche landed in Wichita, Kansas, to refuel. As they were taking off they noticed an Army plane approaching the airport for a landing. Aviation rules stated that airplanes arriving always had the right of way over airplanes departing. However, Louise was in a race and pressed for time. She thought if she continued with the takeoff, the pilot of the Army plane would see them and change course, but he didn't. Louise built up speed and lifted one wheel enough to miss the other plane's tail. In a speech at the Staggerwing Convention in 1973, Louise said, "We saved half a minute, but it felt good—when something feels good, it's alright."[10]

They remained on course until they got to Los Angeles. The visibility was poor because of a thick haze and the setting sun. Louise craned her neck looking for the airport. She assumed they hadn't won, but she was pleased they had made it through the adverse conditions which had caused two of the planes to crash. After 14 hours and 55 minutes of flying, Louise landed, crossing the finish line in the wrong direction. Embarrassed, she said that she and Blanche "tucked our tail between our legs and taxied beyond the grandstands."[11]

They were startled when a group of men ran beside the plane making motions for them to stop. Louise thought something must have gone wrong with the plane. Much to their delight, she and Blanche discovered that they had won—not just the women's flight, but the race itself!

Louise gives her victory speech at the Bendix Race. *Louise McPhetridge Thaden collection, National Air and Space Museum, Smithsonian Institution (SI Neg. No. 79-7388)*

Louise climbed out of the plane in a white suit and blue silk shirt, every bit the proper lady. She and Blanche became the first women to win the Bendix Transcontinental Air Race, in addition to setting a new East-West speed record for women of 165.346 miles per hour. She and Blanche received the first-prize money plus the $2,500 consolation prize—or "special award," as it was referred to in the next day's newspaper. In recognition for her achievement, Louise received the prestigious Harmon Trophy as outstanding female pilot of the year.

In 1937, Louise set two more records—an Inter-City distance speed record from Detroit to Akron, Ohio, in 40 minutes and 43 seconds, as well as a 100 km speed record of 197.9 miles per hour—both in a Beech Staggerwing.

After 1937, at age 32, Louise cut back on her competitive racing. From 1937 to 1938, she served as National Secretary of the National Aeronautic Association. From 1937 to 1940, she was employed as a factory representative for Beech Aircraft Corporation. In 1938, she took time off from flying to spend more time with her family and write her biography.

She continued to work in aviation for the remainder of her life. She was a factory representative for Porterfield Aircraft Corporation in 1941. From 1945 to 1952, she helped in the humanitarian air service called Relief Wings, which was sponsored by the American Red Cross Motor Corporation. From 1959 to 1961, she served with the United States Department of Defense on the Advisory Committee on Women in the Service.

From 1949 to 1970, Louise was active in the Civil Air Patrol (CAP), performing search and rescue missions over the Virginia and North Carolina mountains. One of her proudest achievements for the CAP was the development and expansion of the cadet program, which inspired young boys and girls and provided them with aviation opportunities. She left the CAP with the rank of Lieutenant Colonel.

In 1957, she had the pleasure of flying a military jet, piloted by her son, Bill, a United States Air Force Reserve pilot. From 1953 to 1979, Louise worked for her husband's company, Thaden Engineering, and became the sole owner when Herb died in 1969. Louise died on November 9, 1979, in High Point, North Carolina. Her son, daughter, and granddaughter all became pilots.

Louise contributed a great deal to the world of aviation. She received many trophies, honors, and awards. Many people outside the aviation world have never heard of her, but she is finally receiving some long-overdue recognition. In 1999 and 2000, she was inducted into three aviation halls of fame, including the National Aviation Hall of Fame (NAHF) in Dayton, Ohio. She is only the sixth female so honored in the NAHF's 36-year history.

The enshrinement publication summed it up: "For her outstanding contributions to aviation, her devotion to the advancement of the role of women in all of its aspects, and her performance records that advanced the field of aeronautics, Louise

McPhetridge Thaden is most solemnly and respectfully enshrined by the National Aviation Hall of Fame."[12]

Upon accepting the award for her mother, Patricia Thaden Webb said that Louise never wanted fame and fortune. She just loved to fly. But not long before her death, Louise did confess to her children, "I know I shouldn't covet anything—and I really don't." She paused and, with that twinkle in her eye, continued, "but I do covet being in the National Aviation Hall of Fame!"[13]

Twenty years after her death, Louise Thaden was granted her wish when she received the highest aviation honor given to individuals. Little did she know where she would land when, as a young child, she jumped off that roof with an umbrella.

---

[1]Louise Thaden, *High, Wide and Frightened* (New York: Air Facts Press, 1973), p 9.
[2]Ibid., p. 64.
[3]Ibid., p. 92.
[4]*Phoenix Evening Gazette,* August 10, 1929.
[5]Thaden, p. 87.
[6]Thaden, p. 100.
[7]*Cleveland Plain Dealer,* August 26, 1929.
[8]Amelia Earhart, *The Fun of It* (New York: Brewer, Warren & Putnam, 1932), p. 152.
[9]Thaden, p. 106-107.
[10]Cassette tape, "Louise Thaden: Tullahoma '73."
[11]Ibid.
[12]Enshrinement Program, National Aviation Hall of Fame, July 24, 1999.
[13]Patricia Thaden Webb, acceptance speech at the National Aviation Hall of Fame ceremony, July 24, 1999.

AVIATION RECORDS AND RACES

- Altitude: first official altitude record for women in the U.S., 20,260 feet, Hisso 180 hp Travel Air, December 7, 1928

- Solo endurance: 22 hours, 3 minutes, 28 seconds, Hisso 180 hp Travel Air, March 16, 1929

- Speed: 156 mph, Wright J-5 Travel Air, April 18, 1929

- Only woman ever to hold simultaneous records for altitude, solo endurance, and speed

- Winner, first National Women's Air Derby: 20 hours, 20 minutes, 2 seconds, average speed 135.97 mph, Wright J-5 Travel Air, August 18-26, 1929

- Refueling Duration (with Francis Marsalis): 196 hours, Wright J-6 220 hp Curtiss Thrush, August 14-22, 1932

- Light plane speed: 109.58 mph (100km), 90 hp Porterfield, July 12, 1936

- Winner (with Blanche Noyes), Bendix Transcontinental Air Race: 14 hours, 55 minutes, Wright 420 hp Beech Staggerwing C17R, September 4, 1936; first woman to win the Bendix

- East-West speed (with Blanche Noyes): 165.346 mph, Wright 420 hp Beech Staggerwing C17R, September 4, 1936

- Inter-City distance speed: Detroit to Akron, 40 minutes 43 seconds, Wright 420 hp Beech Staggerwing, January 21, 1937

- 100 km speed: 197.9 mph, Wright 420 hp Beech Staggerwing D17, May 29, 1937

HONORS AND AWARDS

- *Baltimore Sunday News*, Outstanding Female, 1932

- Harmon Trophy Federation Aeronautique Internationale, America's Outstanding Female Pilot, 1936

- Famous Aviators Wall, Mission Inn, Riverside, California

- Civil Air Patrol: Distinguished Service Award
    Exceptional Service Award
    Meritorious Service Award with Cluster

- OX5 Club of America, Broadwick Award—Outstanding Aviatrix

- Citation: The Society of Experimental Test Pilots

- Airport: Louise M. Thaden Field, Bentonville, Arkansas

- OX5 Silver Wings Achievement Award, 1973

- OX5 Pioneer Aviators Hall of Fame

- The Louise M. Thaden Office & Library, Tullahoma, Tennessee, 1974

- Arkansas Aviation Hall of Fame, 1980

- First Flight Society Aviation Hall of Fame, Kitty Hawk, North Carolina, 1988

- Virginia Aviation Hall of Fame, 1989

- Flying helmet taken aboard Space Shuttle *Atlantis*, April 1991

- Award of Achievement, The Ninety-Nines, July 1997

- International Aviation Hall of Fame, San Diego Aerospace Museum, April 1999

- National Aviation Hall of Fame, Dayton, Ohio, July 1999

- Women in Aviation, International Pioneer Hall of Fame, March 2000

Phoebe Fairgrave Omlie

Phoebe Jane Fairgrave was born in Des Moines, Iowa, on November 21, 1902. She grew up to be a small woman who made a big impact on aviation—especially in Tennessee.

While attending the Mechanic Art High School in St. Paul, Minnesota, Phoebe saw her first airplane. President Woodrow Wilson was in town to address the state legislature. St. Paul honored him with a parade and a flyover by the National Guard.

Phoebe was in the physics lab when she heard the commotion outside. She looked out the window and couldn't believe the wonderful sight—not of President Wilson, but of the airplanes. She was immediately stricken with a desire to fly.

During the next year, she was able to save some money, and bought a few airplane rides at $15 each. After she graduated from high school, she got

Phoebe Omlie was one of the first women granted a private flying license and was the first to earn an airplane mechanic's license. *University of Memphis Libraries, Mississippi Valley Collection*

a job as a stenographer. Two weeks later, she received an inheritance of $4,000 from her grandfather, so she quit her job. She had money and knew exactly what she wanted to do with it.

Dressed in an ankle-length sports suit and sailor hat, she marched into the office of the Curtiss Aircraft Company in St. Paul. She wanted to buy an airplane.

In those days, it was extremely rare to see a female pilot. A woman who actually owned an airplane was even rarer. And these men certainly never saw a young woman come into their office, unaccompanied by a father or brother, wanting to buy an airplane. But Phoebe had cash, and money talks. They finally sold her a Curtiss Jenny for $3,500.

Suspecting that her parents would not approve of her spending all her inheritance on an airplane, she went to Fox Moving Picture Company the next day and sold them $3,500 worth of assorted aviation stunts she had devised on the way to their office. The stunts included wing-walking and parachute jumping. Since Phoebe had been a passenger in an airplane only four times previously, she obviously needed some quick training in stunts.

She went to an airport and asked someone to teach her how to perform stunts. The pilot she asked thought (as most male pilots of the time did) that women had no business flying airplanes, so he gladly agreed to take her up in his plane. He executed a series of loops and spins, hoping to see a quivering, nauseated woman who never wanted to fly again.

His plan didn't work. When they landed, Phoebe still wanted to learn how to perform stunts. He refused to teach her. Another pilot standing nearby, Captain Vernon Omlie, overheard her request and offered to teach her.

Vernon had flown for the Army in World War I and, in 1919, had flown the world's first forest fire patrol by air. He started Phoebe with a few practice sessions of wing-walking. She was fastened to the plane with a harness and rope. The first few times they ascended, Phoebe just walked around on the wing. On the third or fourth time in the air, she untied the rope and jumped.

In those days, parachutes weren't strapped onto the jumper's back. The chute was stuffed into a cloth duffel bag and tied to the wing strut. The jumper had to crawl out on a wing, put on the parachute, untie a string holding it closed, and then jump.

Phoebe's first jump was on April 17, 1921. She bailed out of the plane at 2,000 feet and landed in a tree. The local fire department had to cut her down, but she was okay. One time she landed in a lake. She couldn't swim, but the parachute kept her afloat until help arrived. On another landing she wasn't quite so lucky. She landed on high-voltage wires and severely burned her hand, foot, and face.

Once Phoebe had been trained, she and Vernon barnstormed around the country with Glenn Messer's Flying Circus. Barnstormers were pilots who flew around the country to fairs and carnivals and did stunt flying. Phoebe's stunts were a big attraction for the crowds. On July 10, 1921, she set a world record for women when she jumped from a plane flying at 15,200 feet. She was 18 at the time.

Fox Studios filmed her wing-walking, parachuting, and transferring in midair from one plane to another for their *Perils of Pauline* movies. The plane transfer stunt was complicated and dangerous, so Vernon, Phoebe, and her brother Paul practiced it in a barn with a trapeze bar. Paul would hang upside down from the trapeze, while Vernon drove a car with Phoebe standing in the back. As Vernon drove under Paul, Phoebe would grab Paul's hands and swing out of the car, letting Paul support her.

In the air, Phoebe's brother hung from the axle of the upper plane, while Phoebe stood on the wing of the lower plane. The Fox movie camera filmed the stunt in a third airplane.

At one point, a gust of wind hit the lower plane, forcing it upward. Phoebe looked up just in time to see the propeller of the other plane almost on top of her. She dropped to her knees, reached under the wing, and grabbed a strut. Then she flipped over the edge and shimmied down to the lower wing. The propeller of the top plane sliced into the aileron of Vernon's plane, but they were able to land safely.

Fox loved the stunt and wanted them to try it again. The three daredevils went up a second time that day, and Fox got the footage they wanted. But

Broadside of airshow
Memphis/Shelby County Archives, Memphis/Shelby Public Library and Information Center

from that day forward, Phoebe's brother hung from the bottom of a 20-foot rope ladder, making it less likely for the two planes to collide during the stunt.[1]

Phoebe and Vernon decided to leave the Messer Flying Circus and start their own. Phoebe was the first woman to form her own flying troupe, the Phoebe Fairgrave Flying Circus. Vernon was her chief pilot, and in 1922, he also became her husband.

Together they barnstormed across the country. Phoebe continued to make high parachute jumps and even perfected a double parachute jump. After the first parachute opened, she would cut it loose, free-fall for a few seconds, and then open a second parachute. The crowds loved it.

She hung by her teeth from a flying airplane, stood on the top wing of a plane doing the loop-the-loop, danced the Charleston on the wing, and even stood on the top wing while the pilot landed. Phoebe became one of the best and highest paid wing-walkers.

She finally learned to actually fly a plane and, in 1927, became the first licensed female pilot in Memphis, Tennessee. She also earned her transport license—the highest form of license granted by the federal government—from the Commerce Department. She was the first female in the United States to receive this license. She was also the first female licensed as an aviation mechanic.

But income from barnstorming was sporadic, and upkeep on the planes was expensive. In 1922,

Phoebe and Vernon were staying at a hotel in Memphis when they ran out of money, and the hotel seized Phoebe's suitcases.

They had to earn some money, so Phoebe and Vernon gave flying lessons from a makeshift field. They eventually saved enough money to start their own flying school and aviation business, Mid-South Airways, in Memphis.

In 1925, Phoebe, Vernon, and other local aviators formed the Memphis Aero Club. They developed the idea of creating an airfield in Memphis. When Armstrong Field was finally built, Phoebe made her 300th parachute jump at the dedication ceremony.

In 1927, the Mississippi River flooded. Phoebe and Vernon flew over the affected areas to spot stranded people and drop mail, food, and medical supplies. They flew from dawn to dark for eight days. As a result of her humanitarian work, Phoebe was made the first female member of the world-famous Ligue Internationale des Aviateurs, and the publicity made heroes of both Phoebe and Vernon.

Later that year, Phoebe got a job selling and advertising the Curtiss Wright Monocoupe at the Mono Aircraft Company. It was a small plane with medium power, but Phoebe loved it. In August of that year, she was flying with a passenger when he accidentally put his feet against the front rudder bar, sending the plane out of control. They crashed, and Phoebe ended up with a broken arm and ankle.

In 1928, Phoebe was the only female competitor and the first woman to complete the National Air

Reliability Tour. Lasting almost a month, the race covered over 5,000 miles, including 32 cities in 13 states. Twenty-three men competed against her. Although she did not win the race, she received more applause than the winner. She made another first in aviation in the same year when she was the first pilot to fly a light plane over the Rocky Mountains.

Phoebe and Vernon stayed busy with their flight school. Harry Bovay, a Memphis contractor with frequent business in Chicago, bought a Stinson Detroiter, a plane that seated six people, and hired Vernon to be his pilot. They sold tickets for the other seats on the flight, becoming the South's first scheduled passenger service. The plane flew three round-trips per week to Chicago, sometimes taking more than five hours to get there. Each round-trip ticket cost $60. Their maiden flight was on May 7, 1928.

Phoebe and Vernon sold Mid-South Airways to Curtiss-Wright in 1929. Vernon stayed on as manager. In June of that same year, Phoebe broke the altitude record for women. She flew her 65-hp Monocoupe airplane to 25,400 feet over Moline, Illinois. However, the flight turned out to be difficult and potentially hazardous to Phoebe.

During the flight, an oil line burst, spraying her face with oil thickened by air that was eight degrees below zero. She was barely able to see. She started getting groggy from a lack of oxygen, even though she was wearing an oxygen mask.

She later told reporters, "I nosed the ship down

Phoebe and Vernon Omlie barnstormed in the southeast in the 1920s. After settling in Memphis, they helped establish and operate Armstrong Field, the city's first municipal airport. *University of Memphis Libraries, Mississippi Valley Collection*

and started for earth. I guess I was pretty dizzy when I got low enough to breathe well and peek out a little hole in the side of the cabin to see where I was heading."[2] She finally managed to fishtail to a safe landing.

That summer, Phoebe entered the National Women's Air Derby, the first air race for women. Once again, she was flying her trusted Monocoupe. The Powder Puff Derby, as it was nicknamed, was part of the prestigious National Air Race that was held in Cleveland, Ohio.

The race began on Sunday, August 18, 1929, in Santa Monica, California, and ended eight days later on Monday, August 26, in Cleveland, Ohio. The entrants had to fly stock factory models without special installations. There were two categories: light planes and heavy planes.

Phoebe, in the light plane category, was the first one to take off from Santa Monica. Although several women crashed, and one died, Phoebe managed to fly without incident.

Louise Thaden won the race in 20 hours, 20 minutes, and 2 seconds. Phoebe placed fifth overall with a time of 25 hours and 12 minutes. She came in first in the light plane category, and she also won a trophy for having the most efficient airplane in the race.

After the derby, Phoebe told reporters, "As soon as women become more interested, we will have a say and can provide better and more airports, the lack of which has done more to hinder aeronautics than any other thing. . . . We are not flying in this race to interest women in taking a different attitude toward men flying. . . . Flying on a commercial basis is a man's business . . . but women will play an important part in the administrative part of aeronautics."[3] Despite all her achievements, she still thought women had a place, and it wasn't with the male pilots.

In 1930, there was another race for women, the Women's Dixie Derby. The race started in Washington, D.C., and ended in Chicago, Illinois. Like the Powder Puff Derby, it was also part of the National Air Races.

Phoebe flew a red and yellow Monocoupe and led the race from start to finish, making the destination point in 11 hours, 42 minutes, and 21 seconds. Her winning purse was $2,000.

She also entered three other events in the 1930 National Air Races. She flew in the Women's 500 Cubic-Inch Cabin Ship Event, where she won first place and $500. In the Women's Free-for-All, Phoebe placed fifth and won the last event, the Women's 800 Cubic-Inch Cabin Ship Event, along with $750.

In 1931, she again entered the National Air Races. She flew in the Transcontinental Handicap Air Derby from Santa Monica to Cleveland. Sixty planes took off, piloted by 50 men and 10 women, the largest group ever to compete in one event.

Two separate divisions were made because there was a rule that the women and men could not com-

Phoebe christens the official plane of the National Air Race Corp. at Curtiss-Wright-Reynolds Airport, Chicago, June 23, 1930. National Air and Space Museum, Smithsonian Institution (SI Neg. No. 80-19981)

pete against each other. The two divisions flew the same course, and an overall winner was determined based on a point system. Phoebe won with 109.19 points. Her prize was $2,000 and a Cord Cabriolet automobile.

Phoebe was particularly pleased with the rules and regulations of the Transcontinental Handicap Air Derby. She said, "In the two preceding derbies, which we won, we were fortunate in having the fastest airplane in the race. This made it possible for us to ease down on the throttle and cruise most of the way. But here, with a handicap derby, there was an opportunity to try and show the aviation and lay world that the equipment could be pushed to the utmost, and because of its efficiency, along with its speed and endurance, have a chance to win."[4]

For the second year in a row, Phoebe won the Women's 500 Cubic Inch event and a purse of $500. She also won the Women's 650 Cubic Inch race, along with the prize of $750.

In 1932, she was asked by Eleanor Roosevelt to help with her husband's presidential bid by flying a cross-country campaign tour. Phoebe said yes and ended up flying over 5,000 miles for his campaign. In appreciation for her hard work, and in recognition of her aviation skills and knowledge, Franklin Delano Roosevelt appointed her Special Advisor for Air Intelligence to the forerunner of NASA, the National Advisory Committee for Aeronautics (NACA). In 1933, at age 31, Phoebe Omlie became the first female government official in aviation.

In those days, airports were few and primitive, and in 1934 Phoebe became involved in a project that would help to correct this problem. She instigated, planned, and directed the National Air Marking Program. NACA loaned her to the Bureau of Air Commerce for the duration of the program. Phoebe recruited four other female pilots to help her—Louise Thaden, Helen Richey, Helen McCloskey, and Blanche Noyes.

The women traveled across the country and found suitable buildings on which to paint city names, distances, and directions to airfields. Letters were painted in bright orange and were visible from altitudes up to 3,000 feet. The idea was to have a marker every 15 miles. Where towns were too far apart, ground markers of rocks or bricks were used.

The program was very important to Phoebe. She thought in order for the aviation industry to grow as large as the automobile industry, the private pilots must be encouraged. One of the surest and quickest ways to help them along was to mark the country so they wouldn't get lost.

By the middle of 1936, thirty states were actively involved in the program, with approvals given for 16,000 markers at a cost of about $1,000,000.[5] The program was funded by state grants from the Works Progress Administration.

In 1935, Phoebe received the honor of being named by Eleanor Roosevelt as one of the twelve

Phoebe Omlie (left) and Stella Aikin with the Democratic National Committee's plane at Floyd Bennett Field, New York, September 16, 1936. *Rudy Arnold Collection, National Air and Space Museum, Smithsonian Institution (SI Neg. No. 92-7961)*

greatest women in the United States. When interviewed by a reporter about this honor, Phoebe said, "Of course I still fly. But I'm out of racing for good. I didn't do it for fun ever, and I enjoy my present work so much more. It's a great satisfaction to serve an administration which is really interested in the future of aviation."[6]

Things were certainly going well for her. Phoebe Omlie had become a well-known name. She had set aviation records and received national recognition for her aviation program. But tragedy struck in 1937 when Vernon was killed in the crash of a commercial airliner near St. Louis. He was a passenger at the time and only 40 years old. Phoebe quit her job with NACA and returned to Memphis to devote her time to research and development of air safety and flight training.

She joined an old Memphis friend, W. Percy McDonald, Chairman of the Tennessee Aeronautical Commission, and together they authored the Tennessee Aviation Act of 1937. The act took the seven cents per gallon state gasoline tax paid by the pilots and returned it to the state's aviation industry.

Half the money was given to airports for improvements, and the other half was used to finance ground-school training in the public schools.[7] The school program included textbooks, model airplane kits, air maps, aviation bulletins, posters, pamphlets, and booklets. Phoebe instructed the first class in Memphis.

The tax act made Tennessee the first state to make public funds available for training pilots. Their public school aviation training program preceded the U.S. Government's Civilian Pilot Training (CPT) Program by two years.

In February of 1941, Phoebe was appointed the Senior Private Flying Specialist of the Civil Aeronautical Administration (CAA). During the war years, most of the young pilots and airplane mechanics were in the armed services, so Phoebe established training classes for older men throughout the country. By the end of the year, classes were held in 46 states, and 70% of those trained obtained jobs.

In June, the CPT excluded women from their program because all the trainees had to agree to serve in the military if needed. This frustrated Phoebe; she knew women were good pilots and trainers.

Her old friend W. Percy McDonald came up with a solution. McDonald and Colonel Herbert Fox, director of the State Bureau of Aeronautics, had the idea to start an instructor school for women. They wanted Phoebe to supervise the program, and she jumped at the chance.

The Tennessee Aviation Research Instructor's School for Women opened its doors on September 21, 1942. It was the first school for female flying instructors.

The school was funded by revenues from the state's aviation gasoline tax. At the time, there were between 3,000 and 4,000 licensed female pilots in the United States, with 50 of those licensed as instructors. Over 1,000 women applied to the training program.

The women had to have a private pilot's license with 120 or more hours of flying time. They had to be single; or, if married, they could not have dependents, and their husbands had to be in active military service. They also had to agree to instruct wherever and whenever the Bureau decided to send them.[8]

The Special Selections Committee interviewed 15 women and selected 10 for the first class. Six of the women were from Tennessee, and the rest were from Kentucky, Arkansas, Alabama, and North Carolina. Their backgrounds ranged from housewife to aeronautical engineer. The pilot on the committee asked the candidates to do a two-turn spin, and the psychologist asked them how to bake a cake.[11]

The program had several purposes. One was to release male instructors for more active service. Another was to train the women to become ground-school and flight-school instructors. The third purpose was to provide Congress with sufficient proof of the flying ability of women, in order to make them reinstate women in the Civilian Pilot Training Program.

The women lived in Nashville, Tennessee, in an old farmhouse that was initially so filthy that Phoebe had to shovel buckets of dirt out of the closets to prepare the house for habitation. The dining room walls were covered by blackboards and became the women's study hall.

A graduate nurse was in charge of the dorm and supervised the women's exercise and diet. They were also examined weekly by a doctor. They slept on wooden cots with blankets from a local penitentiary. Their uniforms were similar to those worn by the Army Air Force—dark brown coats, khaki-colored trousers, and dark brown caps.

Phoebe was very serious about her students' training. When a flood marooned the school, she borrowed a boat and rowed her students to the airport.

The women spent 12 weeks training 8 hours a day, 6 days a week. Their schedule was full. They awoke at 6:45 a.m., exercised, and then ate breakfast. They marched the mile to Gillespie Airport, where they had a 45-minute class in aerodynamics, a 15-minute recess, and a 45-minute class on meteorology. From 10:00 to 11:30, the women alternated between solo flights, dual flights, and work in the shop. From 11:30 to 1:00, they rested and ate lunch.

From 1:00 to 3:00, there was another period of solo flights, dual flights, and shop work. After another 15-minute recess, they had a 45-minute class on engines and a 45-minute class on navigation. From 5:00 to 6:00, they rested. From 6:00 to 7:00, they had dinner, and their study period was from 7:00 to 9:00, with lights out at 9:30 p.m.[10]

At the end of the 12 weeks, each woman was qualified for a CAA ground instructor's rating in

Class of women flight instructors from Tennessee's Aviation Research Instructor School for women. *University of Memphis Libraries, Mississippi Valley Collection*

meteorology, aircraft structure, aircraft engines, aerial navigation, and civil air regulations, in addition to becoming an "airborne" flight instructor. In case of an emergency, any one of them would be able to manage an airport.

On February 7, 1943, the first class graduated. The graduates were in very high demand. One Florida contractor even offered jobs to all ten of the women.

Phoebe was very pleased with the success of the program, because she thought flight instruction was the best way for women to be involved in wartime aviation. "I believe that women are born teachers. They can serve their country best by using their aviation knowledge to train large numbers of men who can fight in the armed forces. It is the greatest contribution they can make to an all-out war effort—to prepare themselves for and accept jobs as instructors."[11]

As a result of this program, the Civil Aeronautical Administration proposed that female flight instructors train Army and Navy pilots. Tennessee became one of the most progressive states in fostering an aeronautically conscious public.

In 1943, Phoebe became assistant to the Secretary of Commerce for Air, and for the next nine years she served as liaison officer for the CAA while also engaging in extensive safety research surveys.

She quit that job in 1952 for political reasons. She thought the Truman administration was socializing aviation, and she didn't want to have any part in it. She bought a ranch in Como, Mississippi, and a restaurant business in Lambert, Mississippi. Both of them failed, and she lost all her money.

After Vernon's death in 1937, Phoebe had begun drinking, and in 1952, she began drinking heavily. She returned to Memphis in the early 1960s but avoided most of her friends. In 1970, she moved to Indianapolis, Indiana.

In 1975, her aviation friends in Memphis wanted to honor her again, and they finally tracked her down in a fleabag hotel full of vagrants and prostitutes. Battling lung cancer, alcoholism, and poverty, she told her friends, "Sometimes I can't pay my hotel bill and I get kicked out."[12] She didn't want to return to Memphis for any kind of honor.

Phoebe died on July 17, 1975, at the age of 72 at St. Vincent's Hospital. The death of Memphis's first lady of aviation went virtually unnoticed, but the citizens of Memphis did not forget her contributions to aviation in Tennessee.

Ned Cook, Chairman of the Memphis and Shelby County Airport Authority, convinced Tennessee's congressional delegation to write a bill to name the control tower at the Memphis International Airport after Phoebe and Vernon. When the bill was signed by President Reagan in June of 1982, the control tower was officially named the Omlie Tower.

Today, the Omlie Tower stands in tribute to a small, determined, and talented woman who made significant contributions to aviation safety and education, not only in Tennessee, but in the entire United States.

---

[1] Sally Knapp, *New Wings for Women* (New York: Thomas Y. Crowell, 1946), p. 160.

[2] Jim Fulbright, *Aviation History of Tennessee* (Nashville: Tennessee Department of Transportation, Aeronautics Division, 1996), p. 127.

[3] *Douglas Dispatch*, August 21, 1929.

[4] Claudia Oakes, *U.S. Women In Aviation: 1930-1939* (Washington: Smithsonian Institution Press, 1991), p. 15-16.

[5] Louise Thaden, *High, Wide and Frightened* (New York: Air Facts Press, 1973), p. 14.

[6] Knapp, p. 163.

[7] Ibid., p. 165.

[8] Deborah G. Douglas, *U.S. Women in Aviation: 1940-1985* (Washington: Smithsonian Institution Press, 1991), p. 8

[9] Knapp, p. 167.

[10] *Nashville Tennessean*, September 11, 1942.

[11] *Memphis Press-Scimitor*, December 3, 1942.

[12] *Memphis Press-Scimitor*, July 18, 1975.

Phoebe Omlie
National Air and Space Museum, Smithsonian Institution (SI Neg. No. 83-2096)

AVIATION RECORDS AND RACES

- Women's parachute jump record of 15,200 feet, July 10, 1921

- First woman to form her own flying troupe, 1922

- First licensed female pilot in Memphis, TN, 1927

- First licensed female transport pilot in United States, 1927

- First pilot to fly light plane over the Rocky Mountains, 1928

- Altitude, new record for women of 25,400 feet, June 1929

- Winner, light plane division of National Women's Air Derby, August 1929

- Winner, Women's Dixie Derby, 1930

- Winner, Women's 500 Cubic-Inch Cabin Ship Event, 1930

- Winner, Women's 800 Cubic-Inch Cabin Ship Event, 1930

- Winner, Division of the Transcontinental Handicap Air Derby, 1931

- Winner, Women's 500 Cubic-Inch Cabin Ship Event, 1931

- Winner, Women's 650 Cubic Inch Cabin Ship Event, 1931

HONORS AND AWARDS

- First female member of Ligue Internationale des Aviateurs, 1927

- Appointed Special Advisor for Air Intelligence to the National Advisory Committee for Aeronautics by President Roosevelt (first female government official in aviation), 1933

- Named as one of the twelve greatest women in the U.S. by Eleanor Roosevelt, 1935

- Appointed Senior Private Flying Specialist of the Civil Aeronautical Administration, 1941

- Control tower at Memphis International Airport named Omlie Tower, 1982

GLOSSARY

barnstormers - pilots who flew around the country and did stunt flying

barograph - a recording of atmospheric pressure

Beech Staggerwing - two-wing executive transport, used in the 1930s, with the top wing behind (staggering) the bottom one

breaker points - internal part of magnetos

Curtiss Jenny - the mainstay of barnstormers, an open cockpit plane with two wings, used for flight training in World War I

Curtiss Thrush - single-wing airplane

magneto - part of the engine that regulates spark plugs

Monocoupe - single-wing cabin plane, used for racing in the 1930s

transport license - highest form of license granted by the federal government